The Gardening Surprise

Janine Scott

Illustrated by Jon Davis

Emma and Johnny were playing soccer in the garden.
The ball went flying over the fence.
Emma and Johnny looked into Mrs Webb's garden.

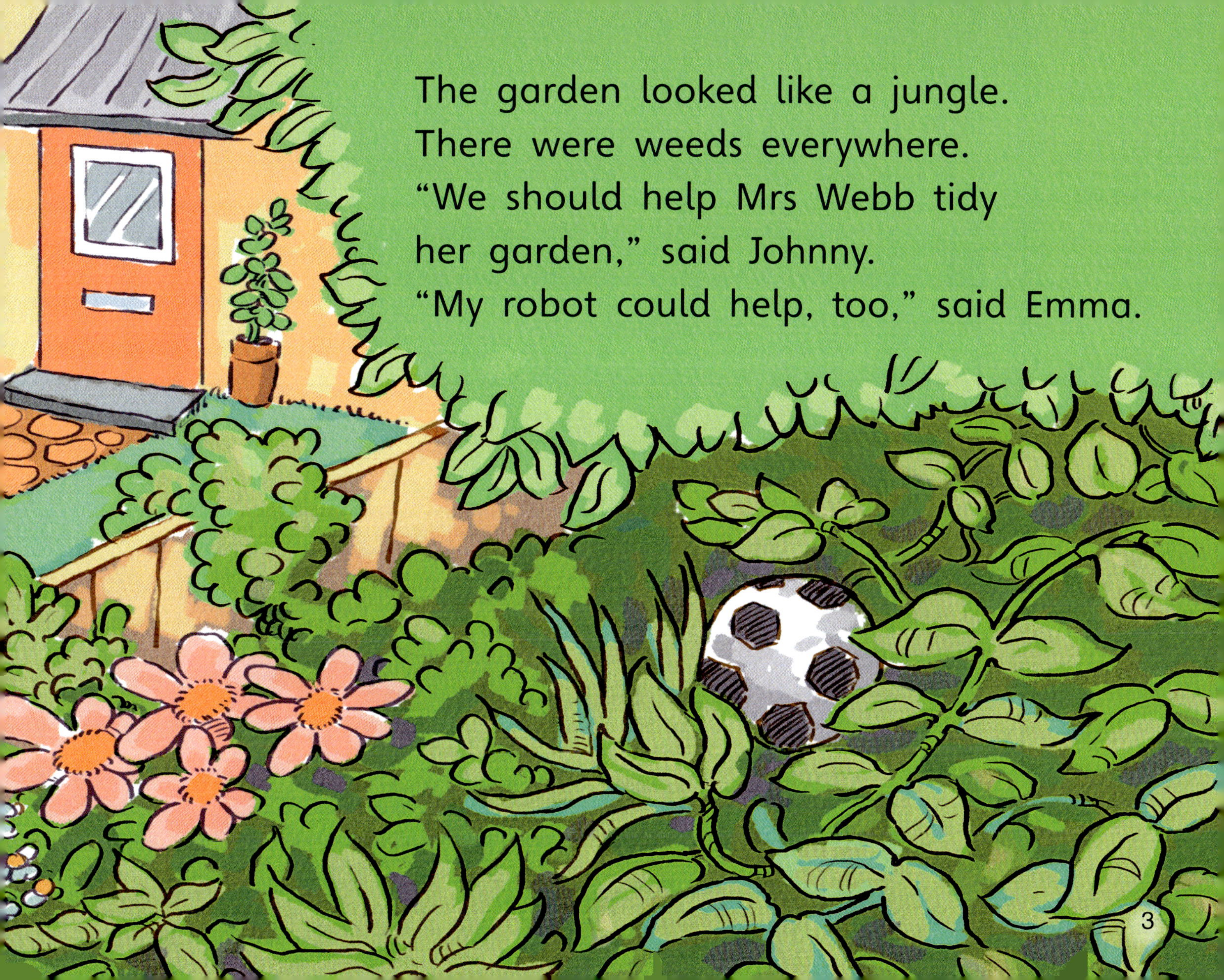

The garden looked like a jungle.
There were weeds everywhere.
"We should help Mrs Webb tidy
her garden," said Johnny.
"My robot could help, too," said Emma.

Emma went into the garage.
She crashed and banged.
She hammered and clanged.
She put a cutting machine on her robot.

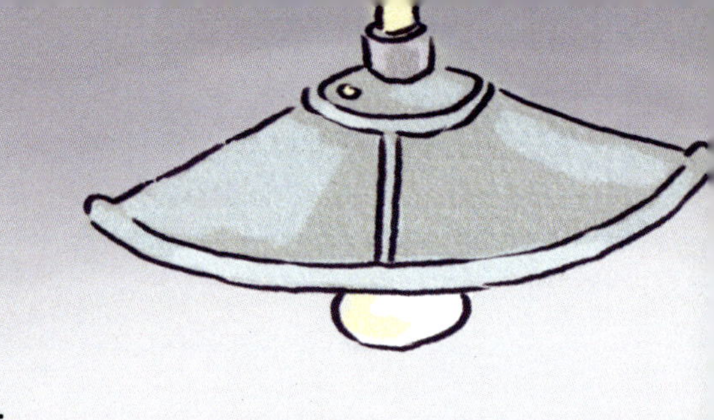

Emma and Johnny went next door to see Mrs Webb.
"Can we tidy your garden for you?" they asked.
"Yes, thank you," said Mrs Webb.

Emma pushed the start button on the robot.
The robot made a buzzing sound...then it got to work.
It swept up leaves.
It pulled out weeds.

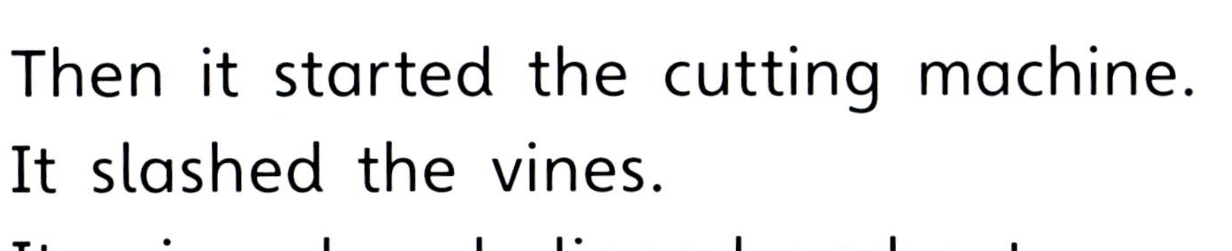

Then it started the cutting machine.
It slashed the vines.
It snipped and clipped and cut.

The robot cut everything it could see.
"Oh no!" cried Johnny.
"Stop!" shouted Emma.

But the robot didn't hear them.
It kept on cutting.

It cut the trees.
It cut the bushes.
It cut the hedges.

Chop, chop, chop!

Mrs Webb was not happy.
“What have you done to my garden?” she cried.

“Don’t worry, Mrs Webb,” said Emma and Johnny. “We’ll fix it.”

Emma ran back into the garage with the robot.
She put a special button on it.
Then she took it back to Mrs Webb's garden.

Emma pushed the special button.
Off went the robot.

Snip, snip, snip!
Clip, clip, clip!

Everyone watched.
"What is the robot doing?" asked Mrs Webb.
"Wait and see," said Emma, smiling.

The robot snipped, clipped, chopped and cut until …

...there were animals everywhere.

The garden looked like a real jungle, and Mrs Webb loved it!